For Varvara and Kolya

ROBOTIKA

SOOK

Written and illustrated by
Alex Sheikman

Colors by
Joel Chua

ROBOTIKA
Written and Illustrated
by Alex Sheikman

Colors by Joel Chua

Published by Archaia Studios Press

PJ Bickett, Managing Director
Mark Smylie, Publisher
Stephen Christy III, Director, Development
Brian Torney, Associate Director, Creative Services

Archaia Studios Press
A Division of Kunoichi, Inc.
3759 N. Ravenswood Ave Suite 230
Chicago IL 60613

Write to:
editorial@aspcomics.com

March 2009.
SECOND PRINTING
ISBN: 1-932386-21-1
ISBN 13: 978-1-932386-21-9
ROBOTIKA is © and TM 2005
Alex Sheikman.
The ASP™ Logo is TM 2003
Archaia Studios Press.

Printed in China.

Table of Contents

FOREWORD

So ... what is this? Simple question, right?

The first time I encountered **Robotika** was an online preview, and to be perfectly honest, what caught my eye was Ryan Sook's evocative cover to issue #1. I've been a fan of Ryan's stuff since I first saw his work years ago, when we nearly ended up working together on a project for Dark Horse.

Now, in the interest of full disclosure, I should admit I'm pretty much a whore for samurai stories. You tell a tale of a taciturn swordsman avenging his slain lord, or maybe being sent on a nigh-impossible quest, I'll show up. So Ryan's cover sucked me in like a moth (or, in this case, a butterfly) to a flame.

But once I got into the story pages, I thought ... "What is this?"

Yeah, there's a samurai. Or at least a taciturn swordsman named Niko. But there's a hell of a lot more than that going on in **Robotika:**

*A future landscape of ecorganic towers and desolate wastelands.
*The very lovely and very bald Cherokee Geisha.
*A cybernetic gunslinger named Bronski.
*Sword fights. Lots of sword fights. This is a good thing.
*Enough tentacles to make Lovecraft proud.
*Naked cyborg assassin babes.
*And, of course, that wacky vertical lettering.

There's also clever storytelling and inviting chiaroscuro art that draws inspiration from Mucha as well as Mignola. There's a little Darrow here, a little Wrightson there, a little Tony Harris everywhere. And all of this springs from the mind and hand of some guy named Alex Sheikman who, apparently, doesn't even do this for a living. Pretty damn good for a dabbler.

So ... we're back to "What is this?" Simple question without a simple answer. You could say **Robotika** is one of those clever hybrids that everybody tries to pull off, but hardly anyone ever does. You could say it's science-fiction, it's a samurai story, it's a Western, it's sexy, it's violent, it's poetic.

But beyond any of those labels, you're about to find out for yourself what **Robotika** truly is: a tale well told. I know of no higher praise.

Ron Marz
September 1, 2006

FORE WORD

If intelligence is the ability to hold two conflicting thoughts in one's head, then Alex Sheikman has got it bad!

The ability to simultaneously hold in one's mind the lure of the unknown and the promise of something satisfying is a rare thing indeed. Let alone convey it in such a way that the listener can't help but be pulled into its magic.

Like most "fables" of the day, everything has to be tied into something that already exists. Toys are based on films, films are based on video games, video games are based on comic books, and comic books give birth to toys. A multi-colored dog chasing its greedy, bloated tail. Albeit, this is only a fraction of today's comics reality. But unfortunately, these days, most do.

What strikes me is the lack of new horizons in a field that is supposed to be all about originality. Pick up a handful of what's out there on the shelves in the good ol' U. S. of A., and you'll see an overwhelming abundance of capes, masks, tights and logos to choke the proverbial gift-horse.

Such is the American symptom. But for sure, they have their place. A place as a part of our societal make-up.

We grew up reading these icons, escaping into their worlds, their stories, and for however long we read we were transported to worlds beyond our mundane everyday lives. But what seems to have been lost, what is so truly obviously vacant in our present-day industry, is the spark of the uncharted. The spark of the "new" and unknown. Stories, characters and places we've never seen or been to before. So new that we have absolutely no idea what they are about, or what makes them tick, or, even still, what or who will be left standing at story's end.

Now, don't get me wrong, bad stories are BAD stories, original or not. Just because something is new, or doesn't tie into anything else, doesn't automatically make it a great, or even good, book. What makes a book good...its core, its focus, a philosophy that makes the reader WANT more. And all the bells and whistles in the world start to sound really crappy if they eventually don't fall into a rhythm the reader wants to listen to.

Robotika has such a rhythm.

A melodic rhythm that enters your psyche and catches your attention. Done without hook or a repetition that gets on your nerves after the first verse, but a poetic violent bloody introspective rhythm that makes you hungry for more.

If you dissected **Robotika** to its core, it's actually an amalgamation of a most unlikely gathering. Robots and geishas, zen and cowboys, apocalyptic sorcery and visceral swordplay. It's enough to make you dizzy with the overload of possibilities.

And most stories I enjoy entering into, either by my own hands or someone else's visions, are the ones that throw everything into the pot, no matter what is right or wrong dictated by what some fabricated formulaic "expert" might say is right or wrong, and somehow pulls from the smoldering bog of disjointed subjects a story with one single, specific purpose:

The beauty of what can be if we allow.

Robotika is such a stew. It's like a broken Victorian lamp, mixed with a pile of thumbtacks, then doused in teriyaki sauce. If you thought about it with common scientific sense, it makes none. But with an open, creative sense of wonder, it all fits seamlessly together.

And THAT is what makes it so amazing to read.

And to see . . .

The art is smooth yet visceral. Clean, yet dark. Upon first glance, it strikes you with its beauty and then rips your chest open with its depth.

Robotika comes during a time when almost everything has such a staid formula to it. But it is anything but formula.

What it is is totally damn brilliant.

Ted McKeever
August 19, 2006

CHAPTER ONE

Ships,
come and go.
People,
just die.

U. Bronski 2098

STORY AND ART

ALEX SHEIKMAN

COLOR ART

JOEL CHUA

EDITOR

BARBARA BARNI

FAR FUTURE...

WITH TECHNOLOGY ADVANCING AT AN EXPONENTIAL RATE, MAN'S NEVER ENDING QUEST FOR PERFECTION REACHED DIZZYING NEW HEIGHTS.

WHILE GENETICISTS ENHANCED HUMANS IN PREVIOUSLY UNDREAMT OF WAYS, OTHER SCIENTISTS FOCUSED ON MACHINES, RAISING THEM TO A NEAR HUMAN LEVEL.

HOWEVER, THE UNIFIED IDEAL OF A TRUE CYBER-GENETIC HYBRID CONTINUED TO ELUDE THE WORLD'S BEST MINDS FOR GENERATIONS.

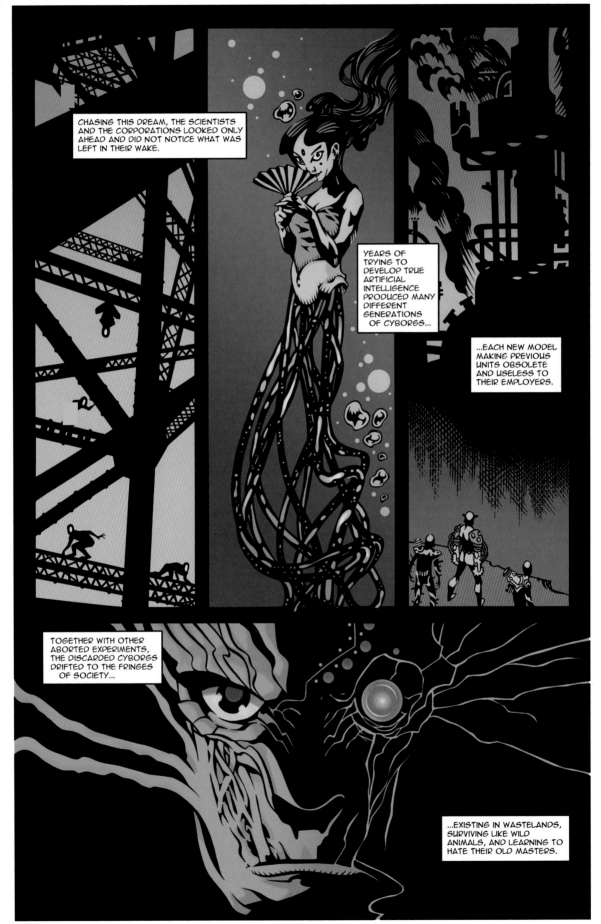

CHASING THIS DREAM, THE SCIENTISTS AND THE CORPORATIONS LOOKED ONLY AHEAD AND DID NOT NOTICE WHAT WAS LEFT IN THEIR WAKE.

YEARS OF TRYING TO DEVELOP TRUE ARTIFICIAL INTELLIGENCE PRODUCED MANY DIFFERENT GENERATIONS OF CYBORGS...

...EACH NEW MODEL MAKING PREVIOUS UNITS OBSOLETE AND USELESS TO THEIR EMPLOYERS.

TOGETHER WITH OTHER ABORTED EXPERIMENTS, THE DISCARDED CYBORGS DRIFTED TO THE FRINGES OF SOCIETY...

...EXISTING IN WASTELANDS, SURVIVING LIKE WILD ANIMALS, AND LEARNING TO HATE THEIR OLD MASTERS.

FAR FUTURE...NOW

HIGH ABOVE THE ECORGANIC TOWERS OF NOVO EDO FLOATS THE MYSTERIOUS LABORATORY OF DR. RHA AGON, THE WORLD'S FOREMOST GENETICIST.

UNBEKNOWN TO THE GOOD DOCTOR, HIS LABORATORY IS BEING INFILTRATED BY THE ELITE MERCENARIES OF THE *BLACK LEGION*.

SELLING THEIR SERVICES TO THE HIGHEST BIDDER, BLACK LEGIONNAIRES DO NOT DEBATE THE MORALS OF THEIR ACTIONS...THEY GET THE JOB DONE.

HE IS CONTESTING FOUR DJIHITS SIMULTANEOUSLY!

IT'S LIKE WATCHING IMPROVISED BALLET. HE IS REACTING TO THE SLIGHTEST SUGGESTION OF MOVEMENT FROM EACH DJIHIT...

...BUT AT THE SAME TIME HIS MOVEMENTS ARE ORCHASTRATED TO CHECK ALL THE DJIHITS AND TO ELICIT A CERTAIN RESPONSE FROM EACH ONE. UNBELIEVABLE!

HE MASTERED THAT SKILL AT A YOUNG AGE WHEN HE JOINED THE TEMPLAR ORDER, WHICH REQUIRES A VOW OF SILENCE. THAT SACRIFICE ENABLES HIM TO FOCUS ALL OF HIS MENTAL ABILITIES ON HIS OTHER SENSES.

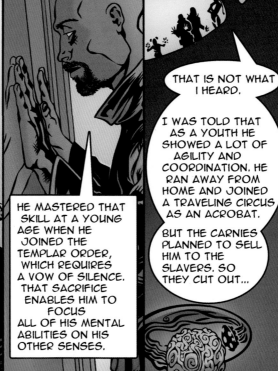

THAT IS NOT WHAT I HEARD.

I WAS TOLD THAT AS A YOUTH HE SHOWED A LOT OF AGILITY AND COORDINATION. HE RAN AWAY FROM HOME AND JOINED A TRAVELING CIRCUS AS AN ACROBAT.

BUT THE CARNIES PLANNED TO SELL HIM TO THE SLAVERS, SO THEY CUT OUT...

...HIS TONGUE, TO IMPLANT SOPRANO TUNED AMPS. HE WAS RESCUED BY THE QUEEN'S CHIEF SCIENTIST, DOCTOR AGON, AND HAS BEEN IN HER MAJESTY'S SERVICE EVER SINCE.

NIKO...

...YOU ARE COMMANDED TO ATTEND TO THE QUEEN...

"...AT THE ROYAL PALACE..."

"...IN HER MAJESTY'S PRIVATE QUATERS."

PLEASE UNDERSTAND, DR. AGON DID NOT JUST MAKE A SCIENTIFIC DISCOVERY, HE CREATED A WHOLE NEW LIFE FORM.

THE FIRST BIOLOGICAL MACHINE THAT CAN REPRODUCE, DEVELOP, AND LEARN ON IT'S...*HER* OWN.

IN THE WRONG HANDS, DR. AGON'S DISCOVERY CAN START A WAR BETWEEN HUMANS AND CYBORGS.

IF THE CYBORGS ARE MADE TO BELIEVE THAT WITH THIS NEW BREAKTHROUGH THEY ARE NO LONGER NEEDED, THEY MAY TRY TO WIPE OUT ALL THE HUMANS AS A PREEMPTIVE STRIKE.

I HAVE DONE ALL I COULD TO HEAL THE RIFT BETWEEN MY CITIZENS AND THE CYBORGS...BUT ALAS, IT HAS NOT BEEN ENOUGH. DR. AGON WAS MY LAST HOPE...

...BUT NOW DR. AGON IS DEAD AND HIS INVENTION GONE.

NIKO, YOUR MISSION IS TO RECOVER DR. AGON'S DISCOVERY AND BRING IT HERE, SO I CAN USE IT TO HEAL OUR TWO RACES.

BUT THERE IS NOT MUCH TIME.

BEFORE AGON'S DEATH, I CALLED A CONFERENCE WITH ALL HEADS OF STATES TO UNVEIL THE DISCOVERY.

I CANNOT CANCEL THE CONFERENCE.

...AND TOPPLE THE MARKETS.

IT WOULD CAUSE GREAT UPHEAVAL...

YOU HAVE FOUR DAYS...PLEASE DO NOT FAIL... ...PLEASE!

A bright and pleasant autumn day to make death's journey.

Fukyu 1771

TO THE NORTH LIE THE GORI ISLANDS. MOSTLY SUBMERGED BY TOXIC WASTE, THE GORI ARE THE REFUGE FOR THE DISCARDED DOMESTIC SERVICE CYBORGS AND ARE CONSIDERED SAKOKU...CLOSED COUNTRY.

IN THIS HARSH ENVIRONMENT, THE EX-GOVERNESS CYBORGS WHO WERE ENCHANCED TO PICK-UP AFTER SPOILED CHILDREN AND TEACH THEM POETRY, HAVE TURNED INTO MECHA-BETSUSHIKIME... FEMALE WARRIORS OF REKNOWNED PROWESS.

W · · E

IT IS ALSO FURTILE LAND OF RUMORS HEARD THROUGH FIREWALLS AND BITS OF INFORMATION DROPPED BY SATELITTE CARAVANS TRAJECTORING TO THE O-MERTO HAN.

NIKO STARTED HIS QUEST HERE, HOPING TO PICK-UP THE TRAIL THAT WOULD LEAD HIM TO DR. AGON'S ASSASSINS AND ULTIMATELY TO THE STOLEN INVENTION.

25

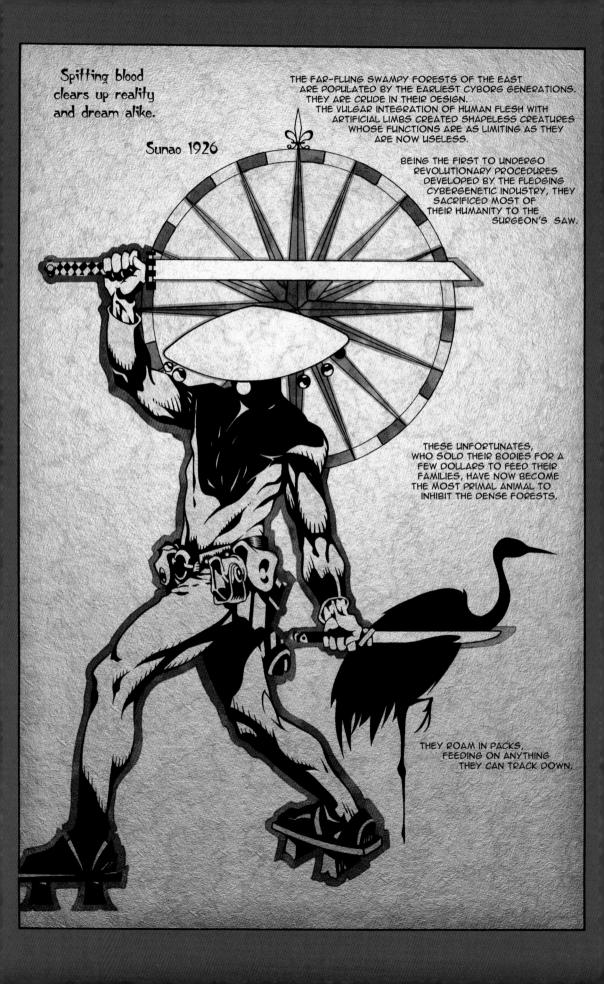

Spitting blood
clears up reality
and dream alike.

Sunao 1926

THE FAR-FLUNG SWAMPY FORESTS OF THE EAST
ARE POPULATED BY THE EARLIEST CYBORG GENERATIONS.
THEY ARE CRUDE IN THEIR DESIGN.
THE VULGAR INTEGRATION OF HUMAN FLESH WITH
ARTIFICIAL LIMBS CREATED SHAPELESS CREATURES
WHOSE FUNCTIONS ARE AS LIMITING AS THEY
ARE NOW USELESS.

BEING THE FIRST TO UNDERGO
REVOLUTIONARY PROCEDURES
DEVELOPED BY THE FLEDGING
CYBERGENETIC INDUSTRY, THEY
SACRIFICED MOST OF
THEIR HUMANITY TO THE
SURGEON'S SAW.

THESE UNFORTUNATES,
WHO SOLD THEIR BODIES FOR A
FEW DOLLARS TO FEED THEIR
FAMILIES, HAVE NOW BECOME
THE MOST PRIMAL ANIMAL TO
INHIBIT THE DENSE FORESTS.

THEY ROAM IN PACKS,
FEEDING ON ANYTHING
THEY CAN TRACK DOWN.

LIKE I TOLD YA BEFORE,

EVRYONE KNOWS WHO HAS IT.

THE PROBLEM IS STAYING ALIVE IF YOU GO AFTER IT.

?

SURE...

CEO OF STARBRAIN INC.

ANDREE LEVI, THE

STARBRAIN IS THE BIGGEST CYBORG MANUFACTURER DOWN SOUTH. THE RUMOR IS THAT MAKING INEFFICIENT CYBORGS IS VERY PROFITABLE... ESPECIALLY SINCE EVERY TIME YOU MAKE AN INCREMENTAL IMPROVEMENT OR DISCOVER A NEW COLOR YOU SELL REPLACEMENTS UP THE KAZOO.

UPSET HIS SALES. WANT **ANYTHING** TO AND ANDREE DOES NOT

HEY...

WHERE...

32

ROBOTIKA

CHAPTER
TWO

Round a flame
a tiger moth
races to die.

Toner 1998

THE HEADQUARTERS OF STARBRAIN INC., THE
BIGGEST AND MOST POWERFUL CORPORATION
IN THE QUEENDOM, IS IN THE ASKINO MOUNTAIN
RANGE. MORE OF A STRONGHOLD THAN AN OFFICE,
THE HEADQUARTERS ARE CARVED OUT OF A
MOUNTAIN TOP.

THE THINNESS OF AIR AT THAT
ALTITUDE IS THE BEST DEFENSE
AGAINST UNSOLICITED VISITORS AS
IT PREVENTS EVEN THE
MOST SOPHISTICATED HOVER
CRAFT FROM REACHING THE FRONT
GATES...AND THE PATH IS
TREACHEROUS BY FOOT.

THE BREAKTHROUGHS IN MEDICINE.......SAFEGUARDING THE ENVIRONMENT....TAKING CARE OF THE OLDER GENERATION...

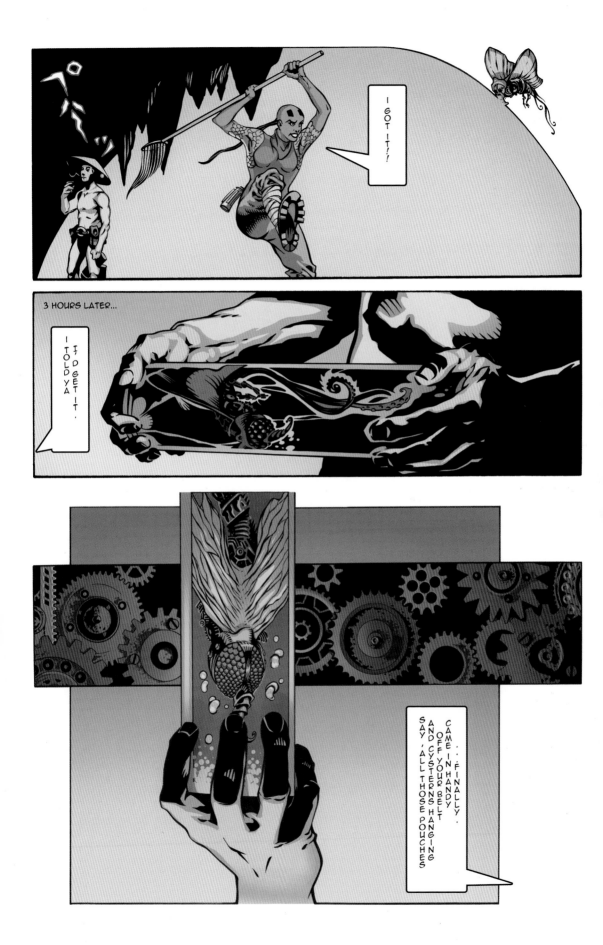

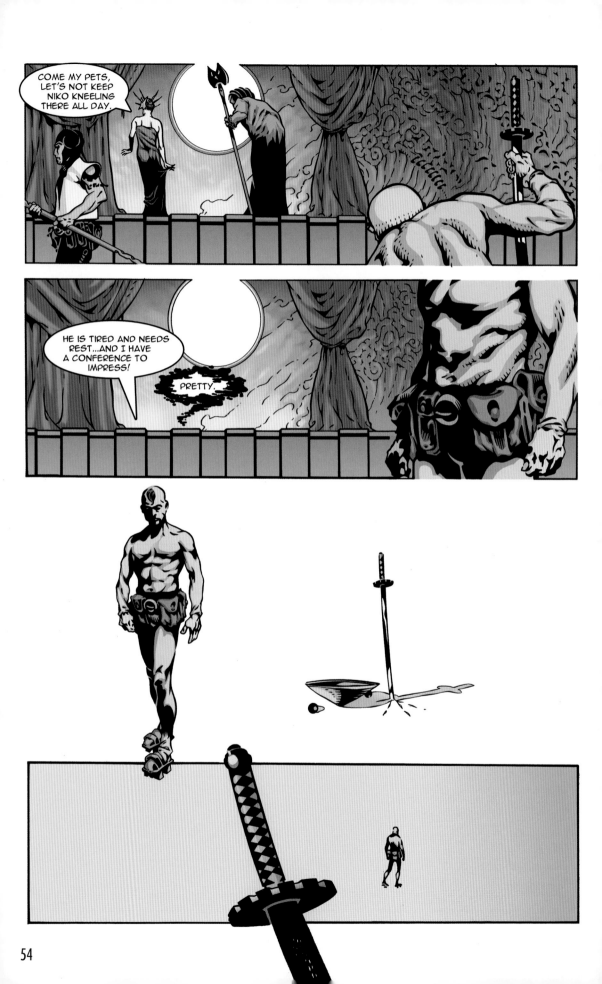

ROBOTIKA

CHAPTER
THREE

WELL DONE, ASANO.
THANK YOU, SIRE.
THE BLADE IS SHARP, BUT WILL IT BREAK WHEN STEEL MEETS STEEL?
ONLY ONE WAY TO FIND OUT. NIKO, AS YOUR DAIMYO, I COMMAND YOU TO DUEL ASANO SO I CAN SEE IF THE BLADE IS WORTHY OF ME.
NIKO, WHY DO YOU NOT MOVE? IS IT TRUE WHAT I HEARD? HAVE YOU REALLY GIVEN UP THE SWORD?
SURELY YOU JEST. MAYBE YOU JUST WANT ASANO....

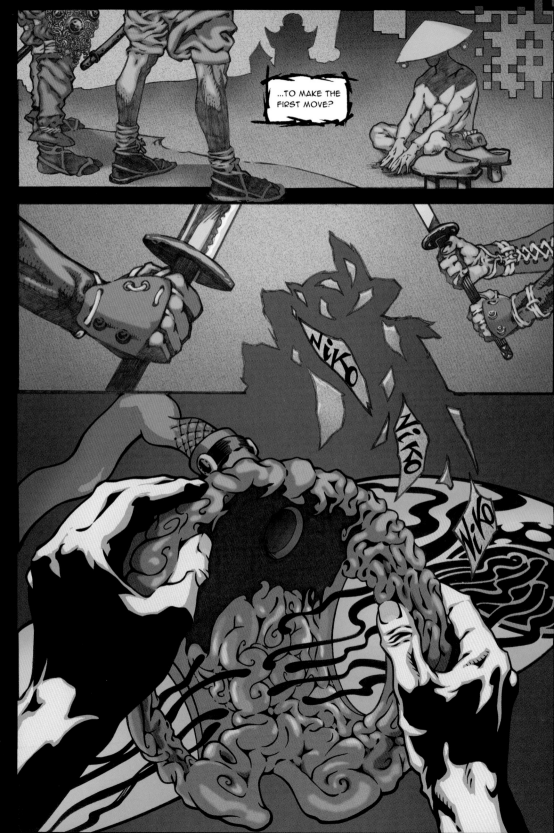

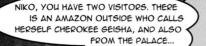

NIKO, YOU HAVE TWO VISITORS. THERE IS AN AMAZON OUTSIDE WHO CALLS HERSELF CHEROKEE GEISHA, AND ALSO FROM THE PALACE...

NIKO, YOU ARE COMMANDED TO ATTEND TO THE QUEEN AT THE ROYAL PALACE...

...IN HER MAJESTY'S PRIVATE QUARTERS.

NIKO...

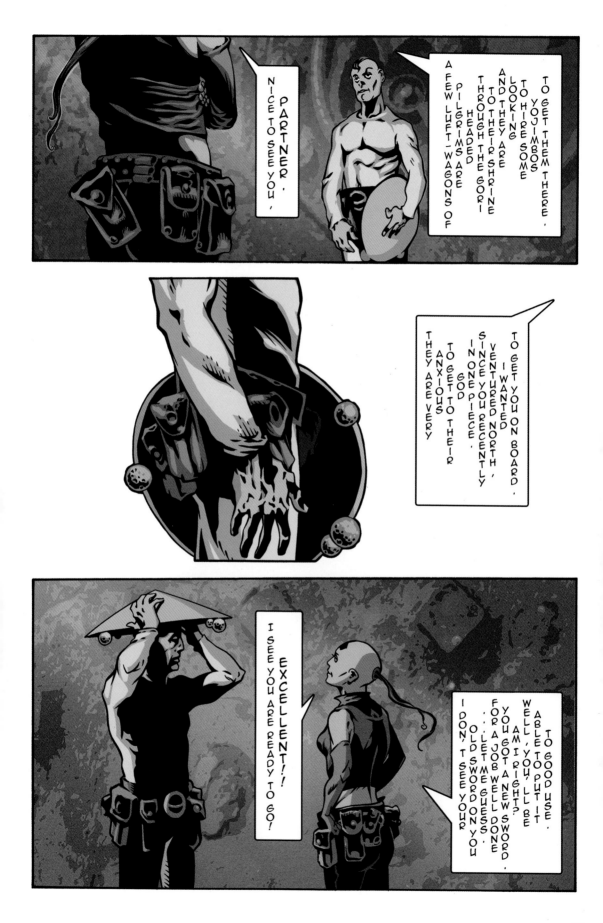

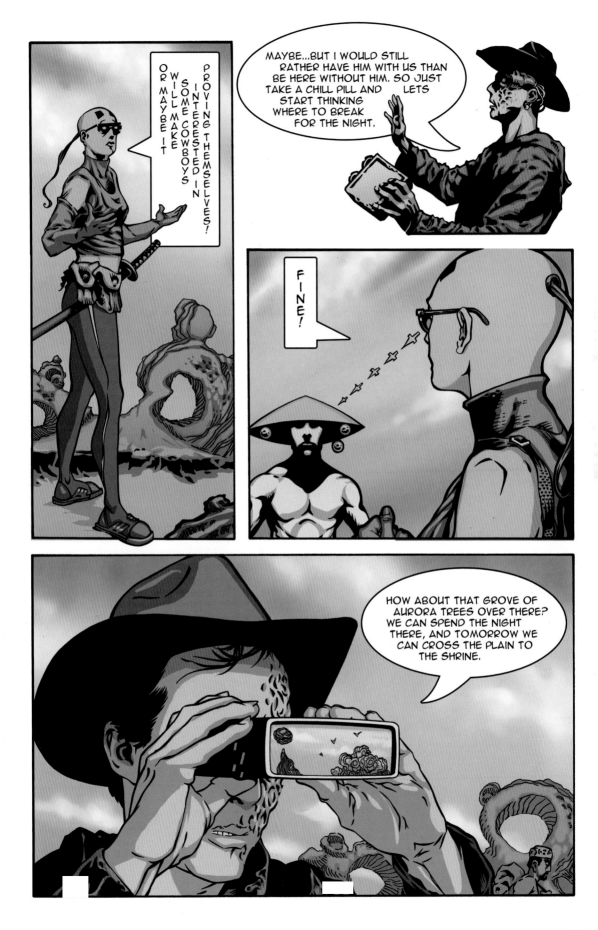

OR MAYBE IT WILL MAKE SOME COWBOYS INTERESTED IN PROVING THEMSELVES!

MAYBE...BUT I WOULD STILL RATHER HAVE HIM WITH US THAN BE HERE WITHOUT HIM. SO JUST TAKE A CHILL PILL AND LETS START THINKING WHERE TO BREAK FOR THE NIGHT.

FINE!

HOW ABOUT THAT GROVE OF AURORA TREES OVER THERE? WE CAN SPEND THE NIGHT THERE, AND TOMORROW WE CAN CROSS THE PLAIN TO THE SHRINE.

FINE!

500 years ago, there was a terrible drought here.

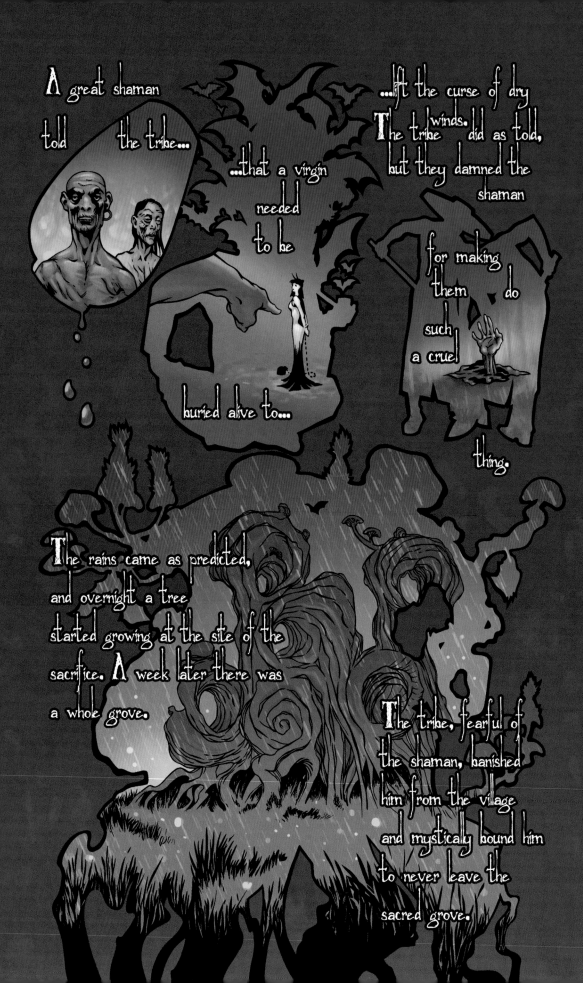

A great shaman told the tribe...

...that a virgin needed to be buried alive to...

...lift the curse of dry winds. The tribe did as told, but they damned the shaman for making them do such a cruel thing.

The rains came as predicted, and overnight a tree started growing at the site of the sacrifice. A week later there was a whole grove.

The tribe, fearful of the shaman, banished him from the village and mystically bound him to never leave the sacred grove.

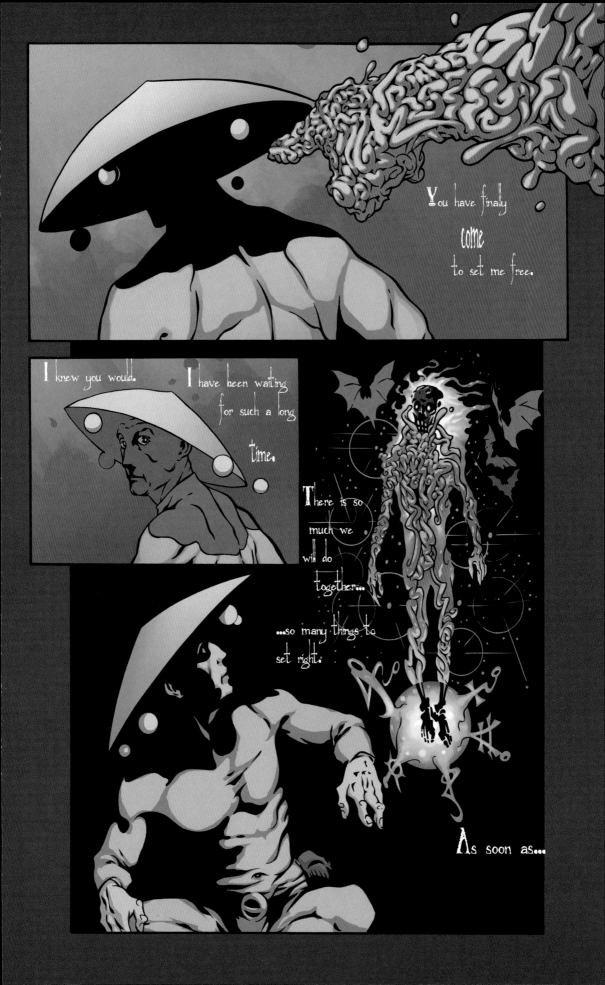

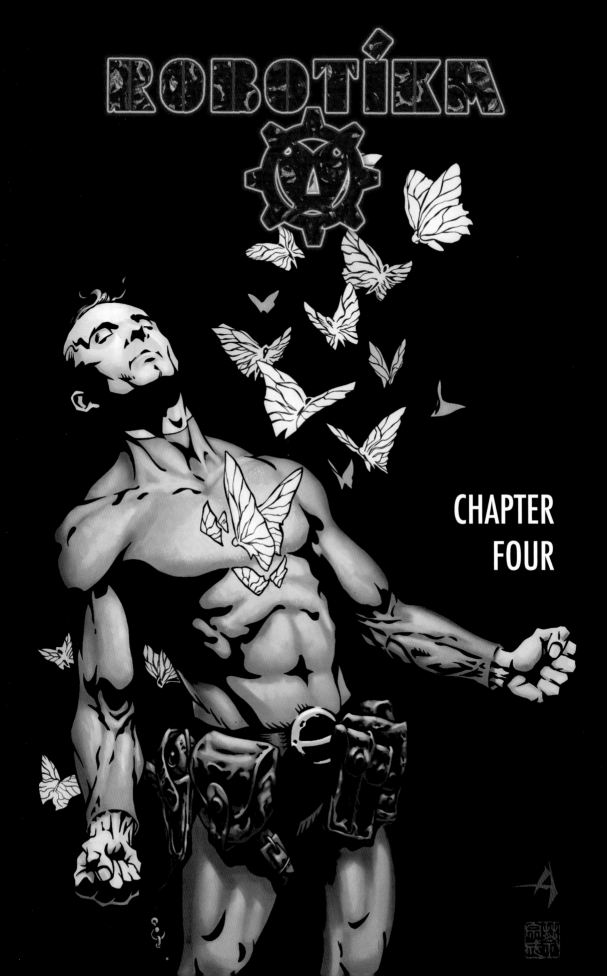

ROBOTÍKA

CHAPTER FOUR

THE *MASTER* OF *SOULS*...

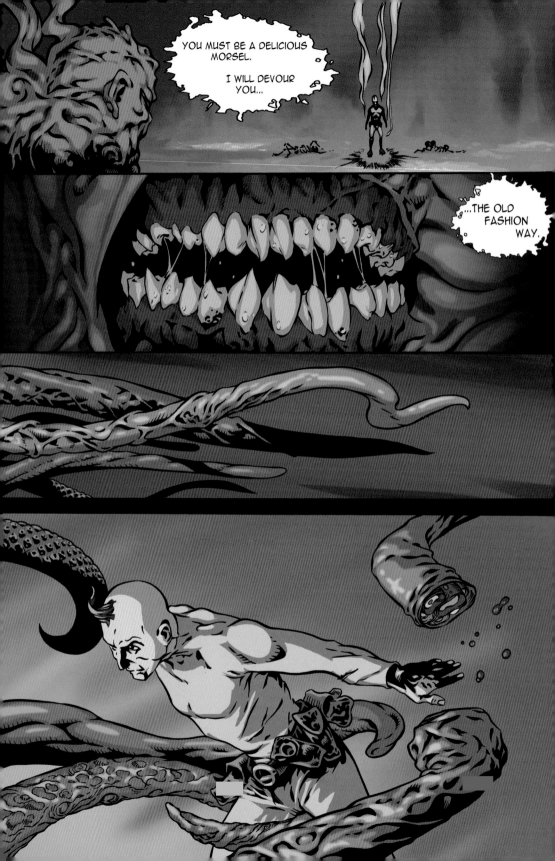

LIGHT AS A
SMILE.

HEAVY AS A
SAD HEART.

HUMAN SOUL.

U. BRONSKI

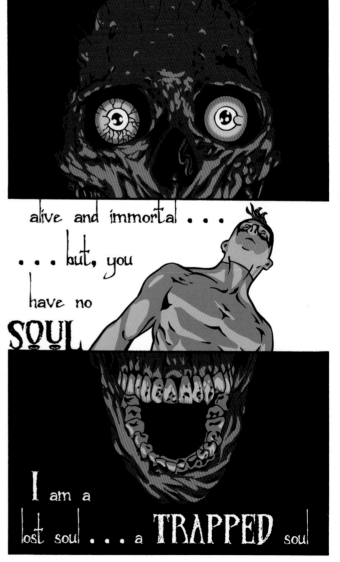

Yesssss...

you are back...

... and now you **KNOW**...

you are everything a mortal man ever dreamed of...

alive and immortal...

... but, you have no **SOUL**

I am a lost soul... a **TRAPPED** soul

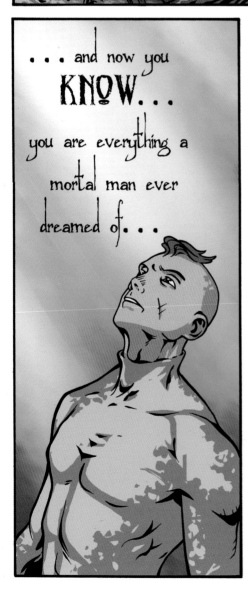

Open yourself to me, I will fill you like an empty vessel.

My body has been damned to rot among the trees, but my soul is intact.

For the first time you will know what . . . .

POWER feels like . . . .

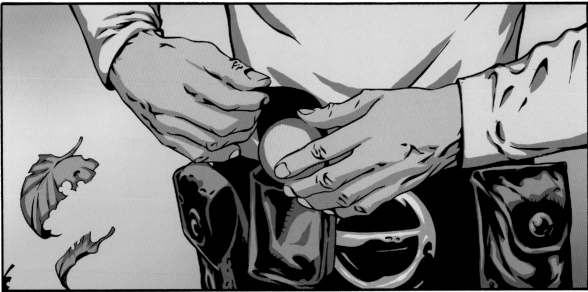

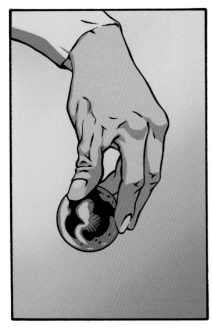

THE WORLD OF ROBOTÍKA

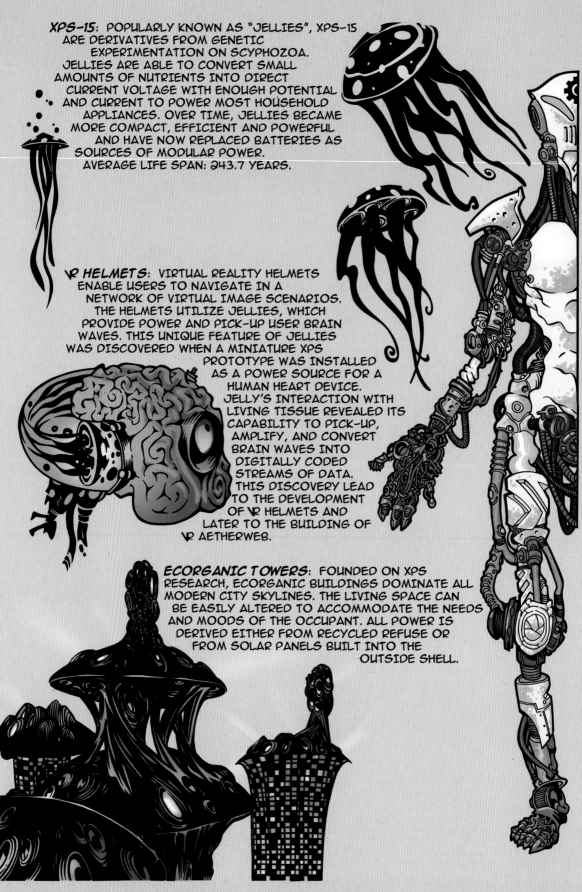

XPS-15: POPULARLY KNOWN AS "JELLIES", XPS-15 ARE DERIVATIVES FROM GENETIC EXPERIMENTATION ON SCYPHOZOA. JELLIES ARE ABLE TO CONVERT SMALL AMOUNTS OF NUTRIENTS INTO DIRECT CURRENT VOLTAGE WITH ENOUGH POTENTIAL AND CURRENT TO POWER MOST HOUSEHOLD APPLIANCES. OVER TIME, JELLIES BECAME MORE COMPACT, EFFICIENT AND POWERFUL AND HAVE NOW REPLACED BATTERIES AS SOURCES OF MODULAR POWER. AVERAGE LIFE SPAN: 243.7 YEARS.

VR HELMETS: VIRTUAL REALITY HELMETS ENABLE USERS TO NAVIGATE IN A NETWORK OF VIRTUAL IMAGE SCENARIOS. THE HELMETS UTILIZE JELLIES, WHICH PROVIDE POWER AND PICK-UP USER BRAIN WAVES. THIS UNIQUE FEATURE OF JELLIES WAS DISCOVERED WHEN A MINIATURE XPS PROTOTYPE WAS INSTALLED AS A POWER SOURCE FOR A HUMAN HEART DEVICE. JELLY'S INTERACTION WITH LIVING TISSUE REVEALED ITS CAPABILITY TO PICK-UP, AMPLIFY, AND CONVERT BRAIN WAVES INTO DIGITALLY CODED STREAMS OF DATA. THIS DISCOVERY LEAD TO THE DEVELOPMENT OF VR HELMETS AND LATER TO THE BUILDING OF VR AETHERWEB.

ECORGANIC TOWERS: FOUNDED ON XPS RESEARCH, ECORGANIC BUILDINGS DOMINATE ALL MODERN CITY SKYLINES. THE LIVING SPACE CAN BE EASILY ALTERED TO ACCOMMODATE THE NEEDS AND MOODS OF THE OCCUPANT. ALL POWER IS DERIVED EITHER FROM RECYCLED REFUSE OR FROM SOLAR PANELS BUILT INTO THE OUTSIDE SHELL.

DRONES: GROWN FROM ARTIFICIAL EMBRYOS, DRONES ARE RAISED WITH SURGICALLY EMBEDDED JELLIES. EACH PAIRING OF DRONE AND JELLY LEARN HOW TO FUNCTION AS ONE BEING FROM AN EARLY STAGE. IN THIS SYMBIOTIC RELATIONSHIP, THE DRONE IS DEPENDENT ON THE AMPLIFIED BRAIN PATTERNS CHANNELED BY THE JELLY TO DICTATE HIS/HER ACTIONS, AND THE JELLY DEPENDS ON THE DRONES FOR ITS NOURISHMENT.

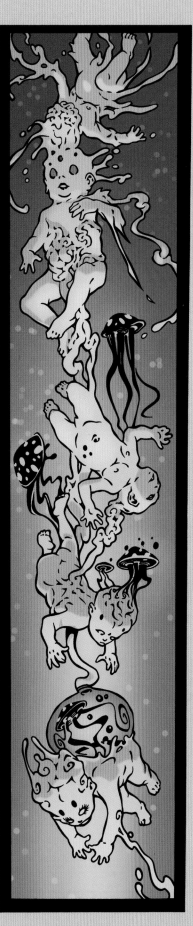

VISION MIRRORS: VISION MIRRORS ARE COMPOSED OF 3 OR 4 PHOTO LIGHT RECEPTORS THAT HAVE THE CAPABILITY OF ROTATING AROUND THE USER'S HEAD AT VARIOUS SPEEDS. THE MIRRORS ARE ALSO CAPABLE OF VENTURING INTO HARD TO ACCESS PLACES. THESE FEATURES ALLOW THE USER A 360-DEGREE PANORAMIC VISTA IN ANY ENVIRONMENT.

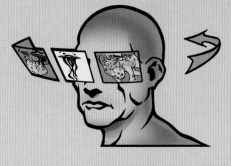

Robotika is a very personal effort, but I believe that a big part of the fun in comics is derived from the collaborative effort of the creators. In order to make **Robotika** as complete a comic book experience as I could, I have enlisted the help of Leif and Travis to illustrate two stories that act as windows into the origins of Uri Bronski and Cherokee Geisha. Both Leif and Travis exceeded my expectations– their interpretations of my script into action flowing across the page has taught me a lot about the craft of creating comics.

– Alex

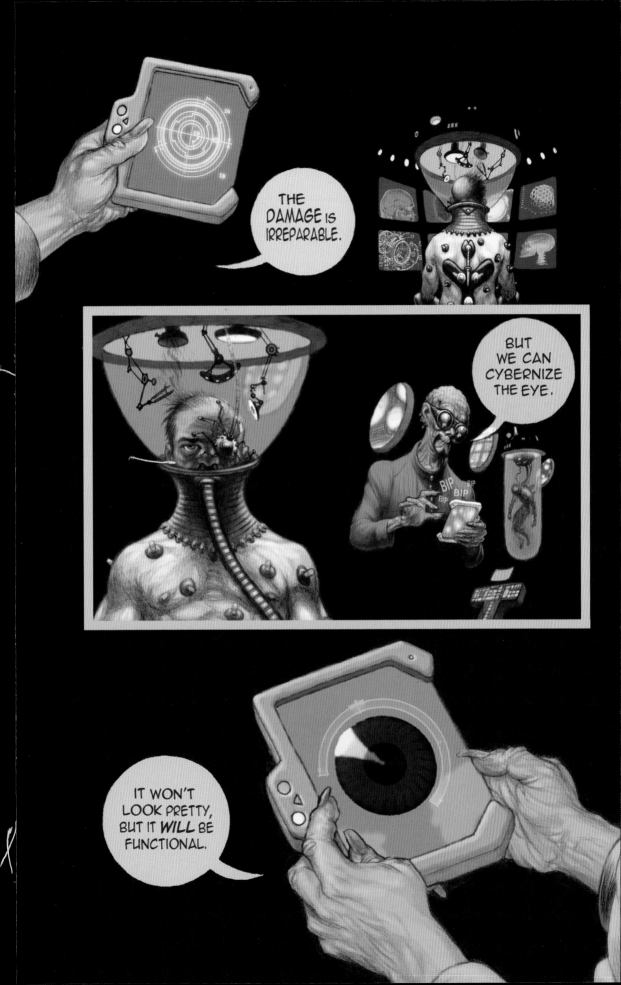

IT WAS A GREAT BATTLE. IT WAS MY FIRST BATTLE...

...AND IT WAS MY LAST BATTLE.

I WAS AN EXCELLENT SWORDSMAN INSIDE THE DOJO, BUT ON THE BATTLEFIELD I LACKED BRAVERY.

HONORABLE WARRIORS DIED THAT DAY BECAUSE OF ME, AND EVEN THOUGH MY SURVIVING COMRADES NEVER SAID A WORD...I KNEW I LOST THEIR RESPECT.

CHEROKEE SONG

Alex Sheikman - Travis Sengaus - Joel Chua

story & inks   pencils   color art

THE NEXT DAY I PLACED MY GRANDFATHER'S SWORD IN A PLACE OF HONOR...

...NOT TO BE TOUCHED BY ME EVER AGAIN.

I BECAME A LOVER ....

...A HUSBAND...

...A FATHER TO A LITTLE GIRL...

...A MUTE LITTLE GIRL.

...AND FINALLY A FATHER TO A BOY, AN HEIR TO MY FAMILY'S

HONOR.

STEAMPUNK SAMURAI

SKETCHBOOK

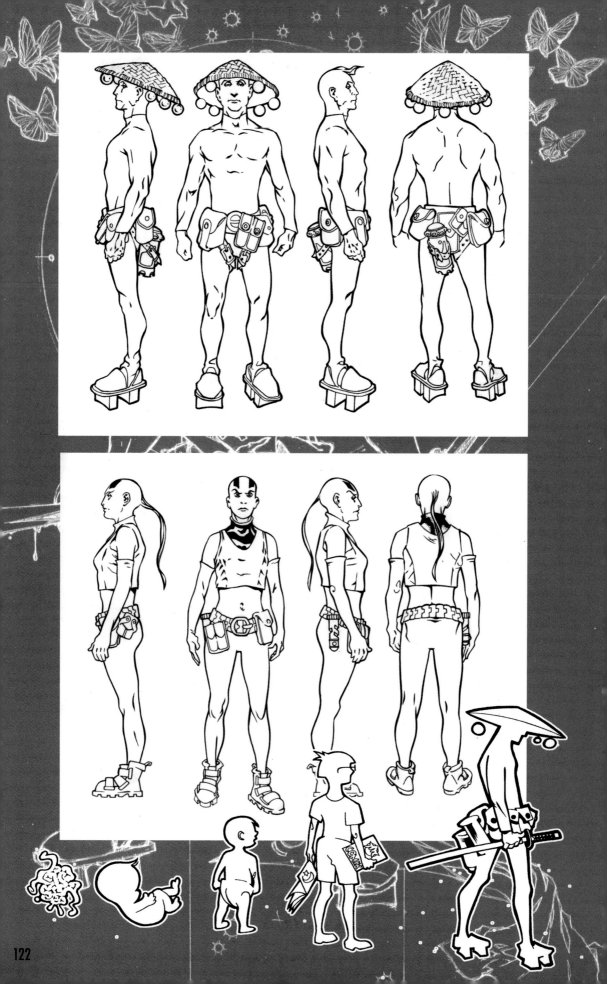

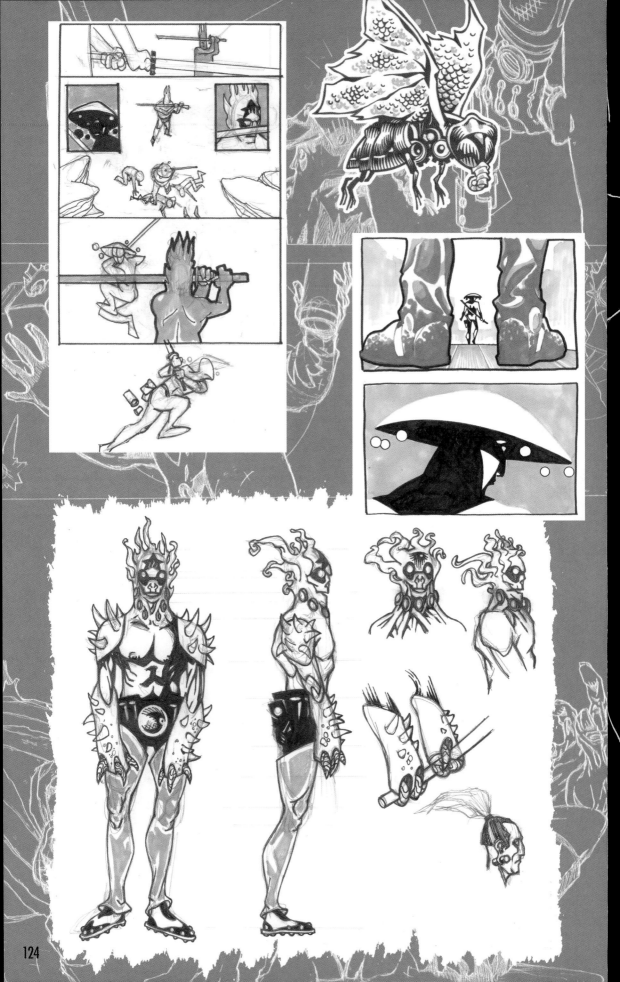